SLEEPY TIME STORIES

Five Minute Classic Tales

Sleepy Time Stories

FIVE MINUTE CLASSIC TALES

Twenty well known classic tales

adapted by

Christine Deverell

· C O N T E N T S ·

Everyone loves a good story!
These classic tales, adapted from the collections of
the Brothers Grimm, Perrault and Hans Christian
Andersen, have captured the imaginations of
children and adults alike for generations. Their
lasting appeal lies in the lessons to be learned, the
triumph of good over evil and the "happy ever
afters"! Adapted especially for bedtime reading,
and beautifully illustrated, these tales can be
enjoyed by today's children.

Jack and the Beanstalk

ILLUSTRATED BY IVANA SVABIC CANNON

There was once a poor widow who had an only son called Jack. He was so lazy he never did any work, and as time went by, they became poorer and poorer. One fine summer's day Jack's mother decided to send him to the market to sell their cow. It was all they had left in the world and even she no longer gave them milk.

Jack had not gone very far when he met an old man. "Where are you going with that cow, young man?" said he. "I am going to the market to sell her," Jack replied. "Well, this is your lucky day," said the old man, "for I will gladly take her off your hands in exchange for these five magic beans. If you plant them, they will grow as high as the sky by tomorrow morning."

Jack thought this was a fair exchange, as it meant he could go home right away and spend the rest of the day lazing in the sun. "Look mother," he cried as he ran into the house, "I have sold our cow for these amazing beans!" "You are stupid as well as lazy," she said as she snatched the beans from his hand and threw them out of the window. Then she sent him to bed without any supper.

Jack slept until late the next morning and when he woke he

was not sure where he was. His room was dark, and when he opened the curtains he saw huge leaves and red flowers covering his window. He dressed himself quickly and ran downstairs and into the garden. Jack could not believe what he saw.

Just outside the window where his mother had thrown the magic beans there grew a mighty beanstalk, reaching towards the sky, so that the top of it was hidden in the clouds. Without wasting a second Jack began to climb. He climbed higher than the tree tops, higher than the clouds until he reached the blue sky and stepped out onto a long, straight, white road. Jack was very hungry by this time, so he followed the road, hoping to find a place where he could beg for some breakfast.

To his delight, he came to a castle, with a very large woman standing at the door. "Good morning," he said politely, "would you be so kind as to give me some breakfast?" "I think you had better run away as fast as you can," said the woman, "unless you want to become a breakfast yourself. My husband is an Ogre who loves nothing better than fried little boys on toast for his breakfast."

Jack was too hungry to run back along the road, so he pleaded with the woman to give him something to eat. "You can hide me from your husband when he comes," said Jack. Now the Ogre's wife was a kind woman, and she took Jack in and gave him some bread and milk. He had only just finished eating when, thump, thump, thump, he heard the Ogre walking down the road. The woman grabbed Jack and hid him in the oven.

The Ogre came into the kitchen and roared at the top of his voice: "Fee-fi-fo-fum, I smell the blood of an Englishman. Be he alive, or be he dead, I'll grind his bones to make my bread." "Nonsense!" said the wife, "you are always saying you can smell Englishmen. Now sit down and have your breakfast." Jack peeped out of his hiding place and was terrified to see what a

huge, ugly monster he was. The table was piled high with food and the Ogre ate all of it.

Then he called to his wife, "Bring me my bags of gold!" She cleared the table and put the gold in front of him. There he sat counting and counting the coins until his eyelids began to droop and his head nodded slowly down and rested on the table; he fell fast asleep, snoring so loudly that people on the earth below thought they heard a thunderstorm.

When Jack peeped out and saw all that gold he knew this was his big chance. He crept out of the oven, and as he passed the sleeping Ogre Jack reached up and grabbed one of the bags of gold. He ran away from the castle and down the straight, white road as fast as his legs would carry him, back to the top of the beanstalk. He climbed down through the green leaves until he reached his own little garden again.

14

"Mother, look
what I have brought
you from the top of
the beanstalk!" Jack
cried as he emptied
the bag of gold coins
onto the kitchen table.

The poor widow was pleased to have her son home again, and now they had money to buy all they needed.

One day, Jack took out the bag and saw that there was not much gold left, so he decided to climb the beanstalk again. He disguised himself so that the woman would not recognise him, and once again she let him in and gave him some food.

The Ogre returned to the castle in the evening and Jack hid in a huge copper pot. Then he called to his wife to bring him his golden hen. The wife brought the hen and placed it on the table. "Lay!" roared the Ogre, and the hen laid an egg of solid gold. "Lay another!" and the hen laid an even larger golden egg. When Jack saw the golden eggs his eyes popped out of his head.

Soon, the Ogre fell asleep at the table and when Jack was sure that no one else was about, he climbed out of the copper pot and grabbed the Ogre's hen.

The hen started
to squawk as Jack ran
towards the door, and
the Ogre woke up.
A few seconds passed before he
realised that the hen was not on the
table, and when he looked out of the
window, he saw Jack with his prize
bird under his arm, running for all he
was worth along the straight white
road. The Ogre chased after Jack
with huge strides. The people
in the world below
thought that they could
hear an earthquake.
Even though Jack was
running faster than he had
ever run in his life, the Ogre
was almost upon him when
Jack reached the beanstalk.

Just as the Ogre reached out
his hand to grab Jack and retrieve
his precious hen, Jack slipped
nimbly down the beanstalk. The
Ogre paused for a few moments,
wondering if this strange plant
would carry his weight. Then he began
to climb slowly down after Jack. The
beanstalk began to sway and creak, and
Jack, realising the Ogre was following,
went even faster. When Jack
reached his garden he called out,
"Quick! Quick!
Get me an axe,
mother!"

He seized the axe, handed her the golden hen, and began to chop at the mighty beanstalk. It swayed and creaked and then it fell with a tremendous crash!

The Ogre lay dead under the leaves. Jack and his mother lived happily all their lives with the golden hen, that brought them more riches than they knew how to spend.

Beauty and the Beast

ILLUSTRATED BY DAVID LONG

Once upon a time there was a merchant who had three beautiful daughters. The eldest sisters cared only for fine dresses and jewels, but the youngest, called Beauty, had a kind and gentle heart, and was especially loved by her father. One day, the merchant was going off on a long journey, and he asked his daughters what they would like him to bring home. "I'd like a fine, emerald necklace," said the eldest. "And a pearl necklace for me," cried the second. "I would like you to bring yourself home as soon as possible," said Beauty, "and if you can find one, I would like a white rose."

The two sisters made fun of Beauty for asking their father to bring her a rose. "You have lots of roses in your garden," they said. "But I do not have a white one," said Beauty, and she wondered why they wanted jewels. The merchant did not forget his daughters' wishes, and before returning home he bought an emerald necklace and a pearl necklace.

But nowhere could he find a white rose for Beauty, for it was winter, and snow was falling. As he was nearing home, the merchant missed his way in the snowstorm, and could not tell where he was. Just as he was about to turn round, he saw lights ahead, and soon found himself at the door of a great castle.

He hoped that they would offer him shelter for the night, and as he went to knock on the door, he saw that it was open.

Not a servant was in sight, so he went inside. In the great hall, he found a splendid supper laid out. He sat down and enjoyed the feast. In the corner of the hall was an open door, and when he looked in, he saw a bedroom that looked as if it had been prepared for him.

The merchant was very tired, so he went to bed and slept soundly. In the morning a fine suit had been laid out for him to wear, and a hearty breakfast awaited him in the hall. He would have liked to thank his kind host, but still the merchant saw no one. As he walked through the garden on his way to the stable to collect his horse, he spied a beautiful rose bush covered with white blooms.

Thinking of his daughter and her request, he reached out and picked a single rose. Suddenly a terrible roar sounded from the bushes and a huge, ugly beast sprang out.

"Who is stealing my white rose?" he growled. The poor merchant trembled and could barely speak. "I did not mean to steal.

"My daughter begged me to bring her a white rose and this

is the only one I have seen." "It is my favourite rose, and anyone who touches it must die!" said the Beast, "But I will let you go if you promise to bring me the first thing that runs to meet you when you get home." The merchant agreed, and as he made his journey home, he hoped that it might be the cat that came out to meet him, and not his beloved dog.

But as he approached the house, it was his little daughter Beauty who came running towards him. He turned so pale that when she saw her father, Beauty thought he must be very sick. He gave her the white rose and took her hand. He told her all that had happened to him and the promise he had made to the Beast. "But I will never,  never give you up Beauty," he said. "You must keep your promise, Father," said Beauty, "perhaps he will not hurt me."

So they prepared to return to the castle. They rode silently through the forest, for they were too sad to speak. At the castle they found the front door open and a meal laid out in the great hall, only this time the table was set for two. They sat down, but Beauty and her father could not eat. Then, at nine o'clock, they heard a great roar and the Beast appeared.

He spoke gently to them, saying to the merchant, "You may stay here tonight, but tomorrow you must go home and leave Beauty behind. Do not worry about her; she will have all she could wish for here." Father and daughter parted with great sadness. But Beauty soon became quite contented with her life in the castle. Her room was very pretty, with roses outside her window, and on a table stood a wonderful mirror. In golden letters around the outside was written, "See your wishes, here enshrined, What you long for, you will find."

28

"I will be able to wish myself home whenever I am unhappy," said Beauty to herself. And she often looked into the mirror to see what was happening to her father and sisters at home, for she spent every day amusing herself, and saw no one until the evening when the Beast joined her for supper. After they had eaten Beauty would sing to the Beast. One night he asked her, "Do you think I am very ugly?" His voice sounded so sad that Beauty found it hard to answer him. "You have a very kind face," she said at last with a sigh, "but you really are very ugly."

A single tear ran down the Beast's cheek, and Beauty felt so sorry for him. "I do like you very much," she assured him. "Then will you marry me, Beauty?" "O, no! I could never marry a beast," sobbed Beauty. She went to bed very sad, and looking into the magic mirror she asked to see her family again. The mirror painted a picture of her old home, and in the corner Beauty saw her dear father lying ill in bed.

Next day Beauty could neither play nor work, and could only wait until supper-time came when she could ask the Beast if he would let her go home for just one week to visit her father." If you go you will never come back to me," said the Beast. "I promise you I will come back in a week, dear Beast. Let me go," pleaded Beauty. "Very well," he said, "but take this ring with you, and if you ever want to come back, put it on your finger when you go to bed, and in the morning you will find yourself here in your own room."

That night Beauty looked into the magic mirror and wished herself home. She fell asleep on her bed tightly clutching the ring, and when she woke she was in her father's house. He wept with joy to see his little Beauty again, and began to get well. At the end of one week, Beauty could not bear to leave her father, so she broke her promise to the Beast and stayed another week.

One night, she had a strange dream. She dreamed that she was back in the Beast's garden, wandering about. As she came to the white rose bush she found the poor Beast lying on the ground, and he looked as if he were dying. As she ran towards him he cried out, "Oh Beauty, you have broken my heart, and I shall die without you." Beauty woke up from her dream and so longed to see her dear Beast again that she reached out for the magic ring and slipped it onto her finger.

When she next awoke, she found herself back in her pretty room in the Beast's castle, just as he had told her she would. Remembering her dream, Beauty quickly ran out into the garden to see if he was there. When she reached the white rose bush she found the Beast lying so stiff and quiet that she thought he was dead.

"Oh my dear Beast," cried Beauty as she threw her arms around his neck. "Please don't die, for I have come back to take care of you, and I will marry you, for I love you with all my heart." She put her head in her hands and wept, and when she stood up, she could not see the Beast. Instead, through the tears, she could only see a handsome young Prince beside her. "Who are you? And what have you done with my Beast?" asked Beauty.

"Do you not know me, dear Beauty?" said the Prince. "I am the Beast you loved and to whom you gave life and happiness. A

witch cast an evil spell over me so that I took the form of an ugly beast, and nothing could set me free until a beautiful girl loved me and promised to marry me." "If you really are my dear Beast, then I will marry you," said Beauty. Together they went to the magic mirror, and when Beauty looked in she saw her father living for the rest of his days in the castle with her. When the Prince looked in the mirror he saw a wedding, with Beauty his bride carrying a bouquet of white roses. Their wishes came true, and they lived happily ever after.

Snow White and Rose Red

ILLUSTRATED BY STEPHEN ANGEL

There was once a poor widow who lived in a cottage with her two daughters. She named them Snow-White and Rose-Red, after the flowers that bloomed on the two rose bushes that grew in front of her cottage. They were delightful, hard working children, only Snow-White was quieter and gentler than her sister. The girls were inseparable, and shared everything they owned. Whenever Snow-White and Rose-Red went into the forest, as they often did, no harm ever came to them.

Birds and animals came
and ate from their hands,
and if darkness fell, and they
lay down to sleep in the
forest, their mother never
grew anxious about them.
The two sisters kept their
cottage clean and bright.

In summer, Rose-Red
would gather a posy of
flowers for her mother, and
always included one red
bud, and one white bud
from the rose bushes. In the
winter, Snow-White would
light the fire and boil the kettle, and every evening their mother
would say, "Bolt the door, Snow-White", and they would all sit by
the fire. The girls would busy themselves with spinning or
weaving while their mother read stories to them. One winter's
evening there came a knock at the door.

"Quickly, Rose-Red, open the door. It might be a traveller who needs shelter," said her mother. Rose-Red drew back the bolt and opened the door. But instead of a man, a big, black bear poked his head in. The girls ran screaming and hid behind their mother's bed, but the bear began to speak and said, "Don't be afraid, I will not harm you; but I am half frozen. Can I warm myself by your fire? "The mother welcomed him and told Snow-White and Rose-Red to come out and sweep the snow from his coat.

Then he stretched himself before the fire and the little girls played with him until it was time to go to bed. The bear slept on the hearth, and in the morning the children let him out. The big black bear came to the cottage every evening at the same time, played with the girls, and slept in the hearth until morning.

But as soon as spring returned the bear told Snow-White that he must leave her, and would not be able to return during the whole summer.

"Where are you going, then, dear bear?" asked Snow-White. "I must go into the forest and guard my treasures from the evil dwarfs." Snow-White was very sad. As she opened the door to let him out, the latch caught a piece of his furry coat, and as he pulled away, he left a clump of hairs behind, and quickly ran off into the trees. Snow-White was not sure, but she thought she saw the glittering of gold in the hole that was made in the bear's coat.

Later that year the mother sent the children into the wood to gather sticks. They came to a tree close to the path, and next to it, saw something bobbing up and down.

As they came nearer, they saw it was a dwarf with an old wrinkled face and a beard a yard long. The end of his beard was stuck in the tree, and he was struggling to free himself.

Snow-White and Rose-Red did not laugh at him, although they thought he looked very funny. "Well, are you just going to stand there? Why don't you help me?" he said angrily.

The two girls tried to free his beard, but without success. "I will run and fetch some help," cried Rose-Red. "People? More people? You are two too many people for me!" snarled the dwarf; "think of a better idea!".

"Be patient," said Snow-White, "I have thought of something." And she took out her scissors, and cut off the end of his beard. The dwarf did not even thank them for setting him free. He snatched up his sack, which was filled with gold, and marched off grumbling, "Stupid people! How dare they cut off a piece of my beard!"

Soon afterwards Snow-White and Rose-Red went fishing. Approaching the lake, they saw what looked like a huge locust hopping about on the bank. They ran up and recognised the dwarf. His fishing line had become entangled in his beard, and a large fish caught on the line would have pulled him into the water. The two girls tried to untangle the dwarf's beard, but they could not. So Snow-White took out her scissors, and cut off another piece.

"You donkey!" cried the dwarf, "How do you expect me to show my face to my own people without my fine beard. I wish you had fallen into a pit on your way here!" Then he took up a bag of pearls, and disappeared into the woods without saying another word.

A few days later the two girls went to town to buy needles and thread. The road passed through open fields with standing stones here and there.

An eagle was flying overhead, and suddenly the bird swooped down behind a stone. Instantly a loud shriek pierced the air, and the terrified girls saw that the eagle had captured the old dwarf and was trying to carry him off.

They did not hesitate to grab him, and they tugged and tugged until the bird gave up and flew away. "Now look what you have done! My coat is in tatters. That's the trouble with you people; always interfering where you've no business!" exclaimed the dwarf in his squeaky voice. He picked up a bag full of precious stones and slipped away to his cave.

By now, Snow-White and Rose-Red were used to his rudeness. So they continued on their errand, and returned home.

On their way past the standing stones they came across the old dwarf again. He was sitting on the grass with his precious stones spread out before him. "What are you standing there gaping for?" asked the dwarf, his face red with rage. He continued to shout and scream at the two girls, when a loud roaring noise was heard, and a great black bear came rolling out of the forest. The terrified dwarf cried out, "Spare my life Lord Bear! Look at these treasures; you may have them all."

The bear said nothing, but lifted his great paw and struck the dwarf with a single blow. The wicked dwarf was dead. The girls were running away when the bear called after them, "Snow-White and Rose-Red, don't be afraid!" They recognised his voice, and turned around, and when he reached them, his rough coat fell off, and there before them stood a tall man, dressed in gold.

"I am a king's son," he said, "but I was cursed by the wicked dwarf who stole my treasures. Now by his death I am released." Snow-White was married to the Prince, and Rose-Red to his brother.

Their mother lived with them, and the two rose bushes were planted in the palace garden just outside her window, and every year they produced beautiful white and red roses.

Puss in Boots

ILLUSTRATED BY JAN NESBITT

Once upon a time there lived a poor miller who had three sons. When he died, all he owned was divided between his sons; the eldest had the mill, the second son had the donkey and cart, and all that was left for the youngest son was the miller's black cat.

The boy was very fond of the cat, but could not see how she would ever make his fortune.

As he stroked her gently, she said, "Don't worry, master. If you do what I tell you, you will see what I can do for you. First, get me a large bag and a pair of boots." The miller's son took the last few shillings he had, and bought the cat a large bag and a pair of yellow boots.

The cat put on her new boots and went out into the garden. She picked some lettuce and put it in the new bag. Then off she went across the fields until she found a rabbit hole. She put the bag down with its mouth wide open so the lettuce could be seen. Then she hid herself behind a low hedge. Soon, a fat grey rabbit popped his head out of the hole. He smelt the fresh lettuce and jumped into the bag to eat it.

Puss-in-Boots immediately leapt from behind the hedge and swiftly drew the strings of the bag together and the fat rabbit was caught.

Then Puss slung the bag over her shoulder and set off in her yellow boots until she came to the King's palace. She presented herself to the King, and bowing low said, "Your Majesty, I have brought you a fat rabbit from the estate of my master, the Marquis of Carabas." The King was amused at the sight of a black cat in yellow boots, but he graciously accepted the gift.

The next day Puss put a handful of grain into her bag and went out to the fields. She set the bag as before and lay down beside it pretending to be dead.

This time two pheasants came and started to eat the grain. She waited for the right moment, and quickly gathered up the strings of the bag, catching both birds inside. Once more she set off for the palace, and presented herself to the King.

"My master, the Marquis of Carabas, begs your acceptance of these two pheasants," said Puss-in Boots, bowing gracefully. "Tell your master," said the King, "that I am pleased to accept his gift. He must have a very fine estate." "Oh indeed, it is, very fine," said Puss as she bowed and took her leave of the King.

As she passed through the great halls, she heard that the King and his daughter were going to drive beside the river that afternoon. Puss raced home to her master, and told him about her visit to the palace, and then commanded him,

"I want you to go and swim in the river and if anyone asks your name, you are to say that you are the Marquis of Carabas." So he left Puss-in-Boots to guard his clothes and went and swam in the river.

54

Puss carefully hid the clothes under a pile of stones, and waited for the royal carriage. As it approached, Puss ran out, shouting, "Help! Help! The Marquis of Carabas is drowning!" The King ordered the coach to stop and sent his servants to rescue the Marquis. Then Puss went up to the carriage, and with his hat in his hand, bowed to the King and Princess and said, "We are indeed so grateful that you happened to be passing just now. But, alas, a thief has stolen my master's clothes."

The King sent a servant to the palace to get a suit, and when the miller's son put it on, he looked just like a prince. "This is my master, the Marquis of Carabas," said Puss to the King and Princess as she graciously introduced him.

"We hope you will drive on and dine with the Marquis." "It will be a pleasure," replied the King, and he invited the Marquis to ride in his carriage.

Puss ran ahead of the carriage and took a short cut across the fields. Back on the road, she came across some haymakers.

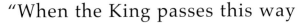
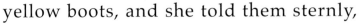

They stared at the sight of a black cat in yellow boots, and she told them sternly, "When the King passes this way and asks to whom this field of hay belongs, you are to say, 'To the Marquis of Carabas, your Majesty.' If you don't, you will be chopped into little pieces."

Then she ran on until she came to a
field where reapers were busy cutting the
wheat. "When the King passes this way,"
said Puss, "and asks to whom this field of
wheat belongs, you are to say, 'To the
Marquis of Carabas, your Majesty.' If you
don't, you will chopped into little pieces."

Now the land really belonged to a terrible Ogre, and Puss-in-Boots carried on running until she reached his great castle.

No one ever visited him because he was so frightening, but when he opened the door, Puss walked straight in, showing off her fine boots.

The Ogre was so shocked that he could only stare at her. "I have heard that you can turn yourself into a wild beast; is that true?" said Puss, calmly. "Well naturally." said the Ogre swelling with pride, and then in a flash he became a roaring lion.

Poor Puss ran and hid herself up the chimney! The Ogre changed himself back again and laughed at Puss, who said, "It is truly wonderful that an Ogre such as yourself can become a great lion, but I very much doubt that you could change into a tiny creature, say, a mouse?"

"Pooh! no problem at all," said the Ogre, and in an instant he had disappeared and Puss saw a tiny mouse running across the room.

She pounced and seized the creature, and with one shake, the Ogre was dead.

At this moment, the King's carriage drew up outside the castle. "You have a splendid estate," said the King to the miller's son, for sure enough, the haymakers and reapers had obeyed Puss, and told him the land belonged to the Marquis of Carabas; "And this is a magnificent castle." They went inside and sat down to a feast.

"This young man would make a good husband for my daughter," thought the King. "Your title does not match your wealth. I shall make you a Prince." The Princess loved the Prince, and he loved her.

So they were married, and lived together happily in the Ogre's castle. Puss-in Boots lived in comfort to the end of her life and she never had to hunt again.

Cinderella

ILLUSTRATED BY BRIAN ROBERTSON

Once upon a time a rich gentleman who was sad after the death of his wife, decided to marry again, so his lovely daughter could have a mother to care for her.

Unfortunately he chose a proud and selfish woman with two daughters just like herself. She did not reveal her true character until after the wedding. She ordered the little girl to work in the kitchen and live with the servants, while she and her daughters enjoyed a life of splendour.

When the child had finished her work, she used to sit in the chimney corner among the cinders; so everyone called her Cinderella. Her clothes were dirty and ragged, but she was far prettier than her sisters in all their fine clothes.

One day an invitation arrived from the palace. The King's son was giving a ball! The sisters could not have been happier. They talked of nothing but what they would wear, and ordered beautiful gowns from the best dressmakers in the land. Cinderella would have loved to go to the ball, and the wicked sisters teased her mercilessly saying; "Wouldn't you just love to dress up in these fine clothes and ride in a carriage to the palace, and dance with rich young men, and maybe even with the Prince himself?"

It was known that the Prince was in search of a wife, and Cinderella's mean stepmother had high hopes for her daughters. Soon, the great day arrived. Cinderella was busy all day, dressing her sisters, polishing their shoes, combing their hair, and when the splendid carriage arrived to take them to the ball, she dutifully arranged their gowns so they would not crumple on the journey.

When they were out of sight, Cinderella sat down alone and exhausted in the chimney corner and began to cry. Then, all of a sudden, her Fairy Godmother appeared and said, "Why are you crying?" "I wish I could go to the ball," sobbed Cinderella. "Well then, be a good girl and do as I say. And you shall go to the ball! Run along to the garden and bring me a pumpkin."

Cinderella found the biggest and best pumpkin and brought it to her Fairy Godmother who touched it with her magic wand. Instantly it became a beautiful golden coach. "Now bring me the mouse-trap, and open it very carefully."

Six mice ran out of the trap, and as the Fairy Godmother touched each one with her wand, it turned into a fine dapple grey horse. Cinderella was then sent to find a rat for her Fairy Godmother to turn into a handsome postilion, and six lizards which became smart footmen.

"Well now, will that be fit to carry a lady to the ball?" asked the Fairy Godmother. "Oh yes. It's wonderful," replied Cinderella, "but . . ."

"Aha! You're wondering what you are going to wear, are you not? Let's see; what would suit you?" With these words, she waved her wand over Cinderella, and in an instant her rags became the most magnificent dress you can imagine. She was wearing the most costly jewels in the world, and on her feet was a beautiful pair of glass slippers. "Off you go now," said the Fairy Godmother, "but mind you leave the palace before the clock strikes twelve, or all this magic will be undone."

Cinderella promised to obey, and set off in her golden carriage. When she appeared in the ballroom, everyone fell silent and the music and dancing stopped, for she was the most beautiful young woman in the room. The young Prince took her hand and led her out to dance with him. He danced with no one else the whole evening.

When they sat down to the feast, he was so busy looking at her that he did not eat a thing! The dancing continued. Cinderella was so happy, she had danced every dance and did not feel tired. Then she heard a clock striking the hour. "It must be 11 o'clock. It cannot possibly be midnight yet," she said to herself, mindful of her Fairy Godmother's warning.

But as she turned and saw the clock, Cinderella gasped with fright and ran as fast as she could from the ballroom. The Prince tried to catch up with her as the clock continued to chime.

As she ran through the door and down the steps towards the golden carriage, she lost one of her glass slippers, and at the very moment that the Prince bent down to retrieve it, the clock struck twelve. As he stood up, the Prince did not see a sign of his beautiful dancing partner; and the coach and horses had completely vanished. Behind a hedge in the garden sat poor Cinderella in her ragged, dirty clothes.

Beside her was the pumpkin; and the mice, the rat and the lizards scurried away. When she was certain that the Prince had gone, Cinderella made her way

home on foot as fast as she could.

The music and dancing would have continued until morning, but the Prince was in no mood for celebration, and all the guests were sent away. He took the glass slipper to the King and said, "I will find the maiden whose foot this slipper fits, and when I have

found her, she will be my bride."

Cinderella's stepmother grew very excited when the Prince arrived at their house. "It's only a shoe," she said to her daughters; "one of you will be able to squeeze your foot into it." But they tried in vain. It was a tiny, dainty slipper, and the sisters had big, clumsy feet. "Are there any other young women in this house?" asked the Prince. "Only Cinderella," said the mother, "but she works in the kitchen, and we didn't take her to the ball." "Bring her here," demanded the Prince. And when Cinderella tried on the slipper everyone cried, "It fits! It fits!" The stepmother and her daughters were white with rage.

The Prince looked into Cinderella's eyes and recognised that she was indeed the beautiful stranger he had danced with, and he took her away to be his bride. They lived happily for many years in the great palace, and the Princess, who later became Queen, was always kind to her servants, and invited them to attend the annual ball.

Rapunzel

ILLUSTRATED BY DAVID LONG

Once upon a time there lived a man and his wife who wished for a child, but many years passed, and they were disappointed. From the window of their house they could see a beautiful garden full of flowers and vegetables. It was surrounded by a high wall and no one dared enter there, for it belonged to a Witch whom everyone feared. One day the woman was looking out of her window and saw a bed of beautiful radishes which she longed to eat.

The longing was so great that as the days passed, she became sick for wanting them. Her husband asked her, "Why are you sick?" "I fear that I shall die," she replied softly, "if I do not eat some of those beautiful radishes that I see when I look out of my window." The poor man thought "I do not want my wife to die, so I must get her what she longs for." He waited until it was dark, and climbed over the wall into the Witch's garden. It was quite deserted, and he escaped with a bag full of luscious radishes.

They were such a lovely flavour that the woman wanted more, so the next evening her husband waited until it was dark, and climbed over the wall into the wicked Witch's garden. As he landed on the grass, there was the Witch in front of him.

"You thief! Come to steal some more of my radishes have you? Evil will come upon you for this!" "Please have mercy," begged the man, "I only did this for my wife, for I feared she would die if she did not eat the radishes she saw from her window."

"In that case," said the Witch, "go and help yourself to all the radishes you want, but there will be a price to pay. When you have a child you must give it to me. I will take care of it and treat it as a mother would."

The poor man was so frightened that he consented. A year later his wife gave birth to a baby girl and the Witch gave her the name "Rapunzel" and took her away.

Rapunzel grew to be the most beautiful child under the sun, and when she was twelve years old the Witch locked her up in a tower. This tower stood in the middle of a forest, and had no door, and no stairs. When the Witch wanted to enter the tower, she called up to the window - "Rapunzel! Rapunzel! Let down your hair." Rapunzel had very long and beautiful hair, as fine as spun gold. When she heard the Witch's voice, she opened the window and let her hair fall down to the ground, and the Witch climbed up the hair to the top.

Three or four years passed and it happened that the King's son was riding through the forest. As he came close to the tower he heard the sound of a beautiful voice singing, and he looked up to see Rapunzel at her window.

The Prince wanted to reach her, but he saw that the tower had no door. So he went home sorrowful.

Rapunzel's singing had so enchanted the Prince that he rode out to the tower every day just to listen to her. One day he saw the Witch come and call - "Rapunzel! Rapunzel! Let down your hair."

The Prince watched as Rapunzel's hair fell to the ground and the Witch climbed up. "So that is how I must reach her. I will try tomorrow."

So the Prince returned to the tower the next day and when Rapunzel finished singing he called out -

"Rapunzel! Rapunzel! Let down your hair".

Her tresses fell down and the Prince climbed up.

At first Rapunzel was frightened at the sight of a man, for she had never seen one before, but the Prince was so kind and gentle that she soon lost her terror.

He asked her if she would be willing to marry him. The Prince was very handsome, and Rapunzel was longing to be set free from the Witch and her lonely life in the tower.

"I would go with you anywhere but I have no way of climbing down from here. Each time you come to me, bring me silk to weave into a ladder, so I can escape."

The Prince visited Rapunzel every evening because the Witch always came in the day, and they kept their secret safe from the old woman. Then one day Rapunzel said to her, "How is it that you find it so hard to climb up to me, when the King's son is with me in a moment?" The Witch was furious. "I thought I had separated you from the world, and now you have deceived me, you wicked child!" She took a pair of scissors and cut off Rapunzel's beautiful golden hair.

She tied the tresses to the window latch and took poor Rapunzel to a desert where she left her to die. The Witch returned to the tower later that day and waited for the Prince to come. When he called out, "Rapunzel! Rapunzel! Let down your hair." she let down the tresses. He climbed up and into the window, but instead of Rapunzel, he found himself face to face with the Witch.

"Aha!" she exclaimed, "your beautiful bird no longer sits in her nest, singing. The cat has taken her away and will now scratch out your eyes. You will never see Rapunzel again." The Prince was so unhappy that he leapt out of the window of the tower.

He fell into a bush, which saved him from death, but the thorns put out his eyes, and he wandered blind, in the forest.

He wandered like this for two years, until one day, he heard a voice, which he thought he knew, softly singing. As he approached, Rapunzel recognised him and fell on his neck.

Her tears washed over the Prince's eyes and he could see again. Together they travelled to his kingdom where they were greeted with much rejoicing, and where they lived long and happy lives. What became of the old Witch no one ever knew.

The Three Little Pigs

ILLUSTRATED BY KATE DAVIES

Once upon a time there were three little pigs, and one summer's day they decided to go out into the big, wide world on their own. As they walked along a forest path they talked about what they would do. "We will each need to find a plot and build ourselves a house to live in," said one little pig to his brothers.

They passed a man with a cart piled high with straw. The first little pig asked the man if he could have some straw to build himself a house. The man was glad to give him straw, and the little pig waved goodbye to the other two, built a house and was very pleased with himself. Soon, an old grey wolf came by, and when he saw the straw house he stopped and looked through the window.

Inside he saw the little pig. So he went to the door, knocked gently and said, in his sweetest voice, "Little pig, little pig, can I come in?" And the little pig answered, "No, not by the hair of my chinny, chin, chin." "Then I'll huff, and I'll puff, and I'll blow your house down." growled the wolf. And he huffed, and he puffed, and he blew the house down, and ate up the little pig.

Meanwhile the other little pigs walked on, until they met a man carrying a cartload of twigs. One of the little pigs said to the man, "Would you give me some of these twigs to build a house?" And the man was glad to give him the twigs. The little pig waved goodbye to his friend, built a house and was very pleased with himself.

Soon, the old grey wolf came by, and when he saw the twig house he stopped and looked through the window. Inside he saw the second little pig. So he went to the door, knocked gently and said, in his sweetest voice, "Little pig, little pig, can I come in?" And the little pig answered, "No, not by the hair of my chinny, chin, chin." "Then I'll huff, and I'll puff, and I'll blow your house down," growled the wolf. And he huffed, and he puffed, and he blew the house down, and ate up the little pig.

Now the third little pig was much smarter than the other two. He saw a man with a cartload of bricks, and he thought, "This is just what I need." So he begged the man to let him have enough bricks to build himself a house, and the man was happy to give him as many as he wanted. So the little pig built himself a fine brick house with a kitchen and a big fireplace. Along came the wolf who knocked on the door and said, "Little pig, little pig, can I come in?" And the little pig answered, "No, not by the hair of my chinny, chin, chin." "Then I'll huff, and I'll puff, and I'll blow your house down." growled the wolf.

And he huffed, and he puffed, and he huffed, and he puffed, but no matter how hard he huffed and puffed, the wolf could not blow the house down. The little pig laughed at the wolf through the window. The wolf made a plan. "If I want to eat this pig," he said to himself, "then I will have to trick him."

So he called, "Little pig, little pig, I know where there is a lovely field of turnips." "Where?" asked the little pig. "Behind farmer Smith's house; and if you are ready at six o'clock tomorrow morning, I will call for you, and we can go together." "Very well. I will be ready," said the little pig. But the little pig got up at five o'clock, ran to farmer Smith's field, filled a sack with turnips and was safely back in his house when the wolf called for him at six. "Are you ready, little pig?" called the wolf. "Ha, ha!" laughed the pig, "I thought you said to be ready at five. I have already been to the turnip field and now I am making a stew for my dinner."

The wolf was very angry, but in a sweet, gentle voice he said, "Little pig, there is a fine apple orchard at Oakwood Farm. Be ready at five tomorrow and we will go together." "Very well," said the little pig, "I'll see you tomorrow."

But the little pig got up at four and made his own way to the apple orchard. He climbed a tree to fill his sack, and just as he was about to come down, he saw the wolf approaching. The wolf called up to him, "Ah, little pig, you did not wait for me. Are they nice apples?" "Yes, absolutely delicious; I will throw one to you," said the pig. He threw it as far as he could, so that as the wolf ran to catch it, the little pig jumped down from the tree and ran home as fast as he could.

The next day the wolf knocked at the little pig's door and said, "There is a fair in the town this afternoon, will you be going?" "Oh yes," said the little pig excitedly, "I love going to the fair; what time will you be ready?" "At three o'clock," said the wolf. As usual, the little pig left home early and made his way to the fair alone. He bought himself a butter churn, and was on his way home with it when he saw the wolf coming along the road towards him.

He quickly climbed into the butter churn, and set it rolling down the hill and heading straight for the wolf. The wolf was so frightened that he turned tail and ran all the way home again. Later that evening the wolf went to the little pig's house. He stood at the door telling his sad tale of how frightened he had been at the sight of a butter churn coming at him at great speed.

Then the little pig laughed at him and said, "That was me inside the butter churn!" This made the wolf very angry indeed, and he growled, "I will eat you up, I will, I will. I am going to come down the chimney to get you!" As the wolf climbed up onto the roof the little pig stoked up the fire in the huge fireplace, and put a pot of water on to boil.

The wolf fell down the chimney and landed in the pot, and the little pig boiled him up and ate him for supper. The little pig lived safely and happily in his brick house for many years.

The Ugly Duckling

ILLUSTRATED BY KEN OLIVER

It was summertime, and it was beautiful in the country. The sunshine fell warmly on an old house surrounded by deep canals. From the wall around the house to the edge of the water there grew large burdock leaves, so high that children could hide in them, and it was here that a duck had built her nest and laid her eggs. She was growing very tired of sitting on her eggs when at last she heard a crack.

One little head popped out, then another, and then another. They waddled out to the edge of the leaves and peeped out. "The world is so big!" they said to their mother.

She counted the ducklings and checked the nest, and there was one egg, the largest, that lay unhatched.

The mother duck sat on the egg until at last it cracked open, and out tumbled the largest and ugliest duckling she had ever seen. "That is a big, strong creature," she said, "not at all like the others."

The next day the sun was shining warmly when the mother duck and her family went down to the canal. Splash! she went into the water, and called to the ducklings to follow. One by one they jumped in, and they swam quite easily.

Even the ugly grey one was swimming around with the rest of them. "Quack, quack!" said the mother duck. "Come with me now, and I will show you the world; but keep close to me or someone may tread on you, and watch out for the cat." They came to the duckyard, where other duck families were gathered. "You must bow to the old duck that you see over there," said the mother duck, "for she is nobly born and of Spanish blood."

The other ducks in the yard stared at the new brood, and then began to talk to each other; "Look how ugly that one is!" they said, and one of the ducks flew at him and bit his neck. "Leave him alone," said his mother, "he is not doing any harm." "Those are fine children that you have," said the old duck, "they are all very pretty except for that one."

"Certainly, he is not handsome," said the mother, "but he is very good and he can swim as well as the others, indeed rather better." She stroked the Ugly Duckling's neck with her beak and smoothed his ruffled feathers. The day did not go well for the poor Ugly Duckling. He was bitten, pecked and teased by both ducks and hens and the turkeys terrified him.

Things got much worse as the days went by; the girl who fed the poultry kicked him, and even his own brothers and sisters were unkind to him. He decided to run away. He ran through the hedge, and the little sparrows were frightened and flew away.

"That is because I am so ugly," he thought, and ran on. He came to a moor where some wild ducks lived. "You are really very ugly,' said the wild ducks to their new companion, "but that

does not matter to us, as long as you do not wish to marry into our family."

Poor thing! He had no thought of marrying. All he wanted was to live among the reeds and drink the water on the moor. He was happy there for two days, but on the third day he awoke to the sound of guns and barking dogs, and the sight of ducks and geese falling from the sky.

He kept very still as the dogs splashed about in the mud, bending the reeds and rushes in all directions. For one terrifying moment, a fierce looking dog thrust his nose into the duckling's face, and then ran off.

"Well!" said he to himself, "I am so ugly that even a dog does not want to look at me."

It was late in the afternoon before silence fell, and the Ugly Duckling waited another hour before he ran away as fast as he could from the moor. As it grew dark he reached a little hut, and when he saw that the door was broken, leaving a hole big enough for him to get through, he crept inside. In this one roomed hut there lived an old woman with her cat who sat on her lap and purred contentedly, and a hen who laid good eggs.

They were all asleep and did not notice their visitor until the morning. The cat mewed and the hen began to cackle. "What's the matter?" asked the old woman, looking round. Her eyes were not good, and she took the duckling to be a fat duck who had got lost. "If this is not a  drake, we might have duck's eggs as well as hen's eggs."

For three weeks the duckling sat in a corner of the hut feeling very sad. One day the old woman opened the door and he felt the bright sunshine on his feathers.

This gave him such a yearning to swim that he could not help but tell the hen. "What is the matter with you?" said the hen. "You have nothing to do all day, so you sit here dreaming. Why don't you lay eggs, or purr, and forget these fantasies?" "Oh, but it is so delicious to swim," said the duckling, "so delicious when the waters close over your head and you plunge to the bottom."

"I think you must be crazy," said the hen, "why don't you ask the cat - he is the wisest creature I know - whether he would like to swim, or to plunge to the bottom of the water. Or ask your mistress. No one is cleverer than she. Do you think she would take pleasure in swimming, and in the waters closing over her head?"

"You do not understand me," sobbed the Ugly Duckling.

"What! do you think yourself wiser than the cat and the old woman, not to mention myself? You ought to be grateful for all the kindness that has been shown to you here. Do you not have a warm room to live in? And are you not lucky to have our company and the benefit of our wisdom and experience? Believe me, I want you to be happy. I know I tell you unpleasant truths, but this is what friends are for. Come on, do yourself a favour and learn to purr or to lay eggs."

"I think I will take my chance, and go out into the wide world again," said the duckling.

"Well, off you go then," said the hen, and he escaped through the open door. He soon found water, and swam on the surface and plunged to the bottom. But all the other animals ignored him: "It's because I am so ugly," he said to himself.

Autumn came, and the leaves turned yellow and brown. The poor little Ugly Duckling began to shiver as the air grew colder. One evening, just as the sun was setting, a flock of large birds took to the sky. They were the most beautiful creatures the duckling had ever seen; their feathers were of a white, and their necks were long and slender. They were swans, and they flew away to warmer climes.

It was a cold, cold winter, and the poor little duckling felt so alone. He very nearly froze to death in the ice, when a peasant noticed him, picked him up and took him home to his wife and children. He soon revived, and the children wanted to play with him, but he was afraid of them, and ran away into the snow again.

It would be just too sad to tell you all the things that happened to him that winter. He was lying beside the canal among some reeds one day when he felt the warmth of the sun on his feathers. The larks were singing and spring had returned. The Ugly Duckling came out into the sunshine and shook his wings. They were stronger than before, and he flew, close to the water, until he landed in a garden with apple trees in full blossom. The sights and the smells were delightful.

Three beautiful swans came swimming proudly along the canal. The duckling was so excited when he saw them that he flew into the water and swam towards them.

"They will probably ignore me, for I am so ugly," he thought, and he hung his head in shame. As he did so, he caught sight of his reflection in the water. And what he saw before him was not a plump, ugly, grey bird, but a beautiful, white swan!

The larger swans swam around him and stroked his neck with their beaks, and he was very happy.

He remembered how he had been laughed at and cruelly treated, and now he heard everyone say that he was the most beautiful of all birds. He said to himself, "How little did I dream of so much happiness when I was the ugly, despised duckling!"

Rumpelstiltskin

ILLUSTRATED BY STEPHEN ANGEL

O nce there was a poor miller who had a very beautiful daughter. He was so poor, he couldn't pay his taxes, and when the King threatened to put him in prison, the miller in desperation said, "I have a daughter who can spin gold out of straw."

"Then bring her to me immediately," ordered the King. The frightened girl was led to a room which was filled with a huge pile of straw.

"Spin all this into gold before morning, or you will be punished." She pleaded to be excused, for she knew that she was

not able to spin gold out of straw, but it was no use. The door was locked and she sat there alone and wept.

After a while, the door opened and in walked a little man. "Why are you sad?" he asked.

"The King has ordered me to spin all this straw into gold, and I don't know how to do it."

"What will you give me if I do it for you?" said the little man. The girl gave him her necklace, and he sat down to

work, spinning the straw into fine gold. By morning he was finished. The King was delighted with what he saw, but he wanted more. So he took the miller's daughter to a larger room filled with straw and told her to spin it into gold by the next morning. Again she sat down and wept.

Soon, the little man came into the room and said, "What will you give me if I do this for you?" She gave him her gold ring, and he worked until morning, when the task was complete.

The King was greedy and wanted even more gold, so the next evening he took the girl to an even larger room, filled to the rafters with straw. He said, "If you can do this tonight, you will be my wife."

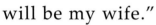

The little man came in as before and asked her, "What will you give me to spin all this into gold for you?" She despaired, for she had nothing left to give him. "Then promise me," said the little man, "your first child when you are queen."

The miller's daughter could only agree to give the little man what he wanted though she hoped that she would never have to keep her promise. The little man spun a huge pile of gold, and not a piece of straw was left. In the morning the King found all he wanted, and the miller's daughter became his Queen.

A year passed, and the Queen gave birth to a lovely daughter. She was so happy that she forgot about the funny little man and the promise she made. Until one day he appeared and reminded her of it.

She offered him all the treasure of the kingdom but he refused to accept it. She cried and cried because she could not bear to part with her little baby.

The little man gave in to her pleading saying, "Very well, I will give you three days, and if in that time you can guess my name, then you may keep your child." The Queen stayed up all night thinking of all the names she had ever heard and writing them down in a long list.

The next day, the little man came to her room and she began to work through the list. Peter, John, Mark, Isaac, Thomas, Henry, Jeremiah . . . But with every name she tried she received the same reply: "No! That's not my name."

On the second day she tried all the strangest names that she had heard of, and some that she made up herself, like Roofabeef, Gug and Boogie. But the little man just laughed and said, "You will never guess my name!" The Queen sent her servants out to see if they could discover any other names.

All but one returned with no new names for her. But late in the evening, as the remaining servant was making his way back to the castle, he heard a little man singing in the woods:

"Merrily the feast I'll make,
Today I'll brew, tomorrow bake;
Merrily I'll dance and sing,
For next day a stranger bring:
Little does my lady dream
Rumpelstiltskin is my name!"

This faithful servant told the Queen of his fortunate discovery, and when on the third day her little visitor arrived, she asked him, "Is your name William? "No."

"Is it Charles?" "No."

"Could it be . . . Rumpelstiltskin?"

"Who told you that? Who told you that?" cried the little man; and he shook his fists and stamped his feet so hard that he made a hole in the floor and fell right into it.

Moaning and groaning, he pulled himself out of the hole and ran away. The Queen lived happily with the King and her daughter, and they were never bothered by Rumpelstiltskin again.

Goldilocks & the Three Bears

ILLUSTRATED BY RICHARD DEVERELL

There were once upon a time three bears who lived in a house in the woods. There was a Little Baby Bear, a Mother Bear and a Big Father Bear.

Each had a bowl for its porridge: a tiny bowl for the Little Baby Bear, a medium sized bowl for Mother Bear, and a great big bowl for the Big Father Bear.

Each had a chair to sit on: a tiny chair for the Little Baby Bear, a medium sized chair for Mother Bear and a great big chair for the Big Father Bear.

Each had a bed to sleep in: a tiny bed for the Little Baby Bear, a medium sized bed for Mother Bear and a great big bed for the Big Father Bear.

One day, after they had made the porridge for their breakfast, they decided to go for a walk to give the porridge time to cool down. While they were out, a little girl named Goldilocks passed the house.

She was not a good, polite little girl, and she peered through the windows and peeped through the keyhole. When she saw that no one was at home, she lifted the latch and went inside.

133

She saw the bowls of porridge on the breakfast table and not having eaten yet, decided to help herself. She tried the Big Father Bear's porridge, but that was too salty. Then she tried the Mother Bear's porridge, and that was too sweet. Then she tried the Little Baby Bear's porridge, and that was just right; neither too salty, nor too sweet, and she ate it all up.

Then Goldilocks sat down in Big Father Bear's chair. It was much too hard, so she tried Mother Bear's chair. That was much too soft. So she tried Little Baby Bear's chair, and it felt perfect. But after she had sat in Little Baby Bear's chair for just a few seconds, the leg broke, and Goldilocks crashed to the floor!

Goldilocks went upstairs, hoping to find a comfortable bed. She lay down on Big Father Bear's bed. It was much too hard, so she tried Mother Bear's bed. That was much too soft.

So she tried Little Baby Bear's bed, and it felt perfect. She got right under the covers and fell fast asleep.

While she slept, the three bears came home for their breakfast. Goldilocks had made quite a mess on the table.

"Who's been eating my porridge?" boomed Big Father Bear in his great, gruff voice. "Who's been eating my porridge?" said Mother Bear in her cross voice. "And who's been eating my porridge?" cried Little Baby Bear in his squeaky little voice, "And they've eaten it all up!"

They looked around the room and saw that the furniture had been moved. They went over to their chairs. "Who's been sitting on my chair?" boomed Big Father Bear in his great, gruff voice. For Goldilocks had used the hard cushion to wipe the porridge off her fingers. "Who's been sitting on my chair?" said Mother Bear in her cross voice. For Goldilocks had left a big dent in the soft cushion. "And who's been sitting on my chair?" cried Little Baby Bear in his squeaky little voice, "And they've broken it!" By now poor Little Baby Bear was in tears.

Together the three bears went upstairs to the bedroom. First, they came to Big Father Bear's bed. "Who's been lying on my bed?" boomed Big Father Bear in his great, gruff voice. For Goldilocks had crumpled the sheets. "Who's been lying on my bed?" said Mother Bear in her cross voice. For Goldilocks had thrown the soft pillows onto the floor, and left a dirty mark on the fine quilt.

"And who is that sleeping in my bed?" cried Little Baby Bear in his squeaky little voice through his tears. "Look! She ate my porridge! She broke my chair! She made a mess in our house! And now, there she is! She's sleeping in my bed!"

Suddenly, Goldilocks woke up and saw the three bears staring down at her crossly. She sprung out of the bed and sped down the stairs, out of the front door and into the wood. The three bears heard Goldilocks crying out: "There's bears in the wood! Help! Help! There's bears in the wood!" Her voice faded into silence, and the three bears were never bothered by her again.

Little Red Riding Hood

ILLUSTRATED BY DAVID LONG

A very long time ago, so many wild beasts prowled about in the forests that no one was ever surprised to meet a wolf or a bear. A little girl, whom everyone called Red Riding Hood, lived in a cottage on the edge of a wood with her mother and father, who worked as a woodcutter. Red Riding Hood was not her real name, but it was given her because she always wore a red hooded coat that her grandmother had made for her.

Now this grandmother lived alone in a rose covered cottage on the other side of the wood, and Red Riding Hood loved to visit her. One day little girl's mother called her and said, "Why don't you go to your grandmother's house for tea today? She has not been well, so I have baked her a cake and made her some lemonade." Handing her the gifts in a basket she added, "Do not stray from the path and do not stop to talk to anyone on the way."

Red Riding Hood promised to go straight to the cottage; so her mother tied on her red hood, kissed her goodbye, and off she went.

She had not gone very far along the path when she met a wolf. "Good morning, Little Red Riding Hood, where are you

going today?" he asked her. "Good morning Mr Wolf" she said, politely, "I am going to visit my grandmother." "And what are you carrying in the basket?" asked the wolf.

"Cake and lemonade for our tea," Little Red Riding Hood replied. "So where does your grandmother live?" asked the wolf

in his sweetest voice. "I continue along this path, take the left path when it divides in two, and walk for another ten minutes.

It's the cottage that is covered with roses." "Aha, your grandmother likes flowers, does she? Why don't you pick some of these from beside the path and take them to her?" suggested the wolf.

Then the wolf trotted off, and Little Red Riding Hood thought it would be a great idea to gather a posy for her grandmother.

First, she picked a few flowers from beside the path, but then she saw that there were some prettier ones under the trees. So she disobeyed her mother's command, and stepped off the path.

The sun was shining through the branches and birds were singing happily. Little Red Riding Hood suddenly remembered that she should have kept to the path and gone straight to her grandmother's cottage, so she picked up her basket and the bunch of flowers, and set off once again.

Meanwhile, the wolf had raced ahead, following Little Red Riding Hood's directions to the cottage. "The rose covered cottage, she said, so this must be it. Aha!"he said to himself, "Now I shall gobble up the old grandmother, and I'll have Little Red Riding Hood for dessert." He knocked on the door very gently. "Lift the latch and come in." said the old lady. The wolf lifted the latch and burst through the door, and gobbled up the poor old grandmother in

one mouthful. Then he found one of her big frilly nightcaps in a drawer, pulled it over his ears and jumped into bed, taking care to draw the sheet well up under his chin. A few moments later Red Riding Hood tapped on the door of the cottage.

151

"Lift the latch and come in," said the wolf in his softest voice. But this voice did not sound like Little Red Riding Hood's grandmother, and the little girl wondered what was wrong. "Mother

has sent some cake and lemonade for our tea, but grandmother, how strange your voice sounds, and why are you in bed?"

"I have a cold on my chest," answered the wolf. "Come here, my dear and sit on the bed." As Red Riding Hood approached the bed, she could not believe what she saw.

"Oh Grandmother, what big eyes you have!" she said.

"All the better to see you with my dear," answered the wolf.

"But Grandmother, what big ears you have."

"All the better to hear you with, my dear."

"But Grandmother, what big teeth you have."

"All the better to gobble you up with my dear," said the wolf as he leapt out of the bed.

Little Red Riding Hood turned and ran screaming towards the door.

The wolf had just caught her red cloak in his mouth when
the door burst open, and Little Red Riding Hood's own father
came rushing in.

With one blow of his axe he struck the wicked wolf dead,
and picked up Little Red Riding Hood in his arms and hugged her.

"Oh Father, I think the wolf must have eaten up dear
Grandmother," sobbed Little Red Riding Hood. So he took out
his knife, and carefully cut the wolf open. Inside, they found the
old Grandmother safe and sound, for the wolf in his greed had
swallowed her whole, and his teeth had not touched her.

They all sat down to enjoy their cake and lemonade, and Little Red Riding Hood promised that she would never talk to any wolf that she might meet in the woods, and she would always obey her mother and never stray from the path.

Sleeping Beauty

ILLUSTRATED BY JAN NESBITT

A long time ago there lived a King and Queen who were very sad, because they had no children. One day, as the Queen sat by a pond in the castle gardens thinking of her wishes, a frog hopped on to a lily pad in front of her and said, "Your wish will be granted. Before a year has passed, you shall have a daughter."

Everything happened as the frog had said. A little girl was born, and the King was so happy that he ordered a great celebration feast to be held. All their friends and relatives, and Kings and Queens from other kingdoms were invited, together with twelve fairies who would bring special gifts to the Princess.

Now it happened that there were thirteen such fairies living in this domain, and everyone knows that thirteen is an unlucky number. So one of these was not invited to the feast, and she was not a happy fairy. The day for the feast arrived and all the guests were gathered in the Great Hall of the King's castle. Every guest brought a gift, and the twelve fairies lined up to bestow their special gifts on the baby.

"I give her virtue," said one. "I give her beauty," said another. Yet another gave her riches, another health and so on, until she had all the gifts that any mother or father could wish their child to own. Eleven fairies gave their gifts, and as the twelfth stepped forward, the door flew open, and in marched the thirteenth who was determined to have her revenge.

"On her fifteenth birthday the Princess shall prick her finger on a needle and die!" she exclaimed loudly, and turned her back on the whole company and left. Then the twelfth fairy, who had not yet given her gift, stepped forward. She said that she could not undo the wicked fairy's curse, but she could soften it.

"The King's daughter will not die, but will sleep for a hundred years." But the King and Queen hoped to save their daughter from this fate, and ordered that all the needles in the Kingdom should be destroyed.

The Princess grew to be beautiful, wise, friendly and well behaved. Everyone who knew her, loved her.

Now it happened that on the morning of the day of her fifteenth birthday, the King and Queen were not at home, so the Princess was alone in the castle.

She wandered around from room to room, along the corridors and up and down the splendid staircases until she came upon an old tower. She climbed the narrow, winding stairs until she reached a door, in the lock of which was a rusty key. The Princess turned the key, the door sprang open, and there in the room she saw an old woman with a spinning wheel. "Good morning, my good lady," said the Princess, "what are you doing here?" "I am spinning," she replied, "here, you can try it."

No sooner had she taken hold of the spindle, the Princess pricked her finger and fell back onto a bed in a deep sleep. Everyone in the castle fell asleep; The King and Queen who had just returned home, their courtiers and servants. The horses in the stable, the doves on the roof, the flies on the walls, and even the fire in the hearth all appeared to die in the same moment.

A thick bramble hedge quickly grew around the castle until not even the flag on the high tower could be seen. The story was told throughout many lands of the beautiful Princess asleep in a lost castle where every living creature lay motionless.

Many princes came and tried to cut their way through the thorns to reach her, but they were unsuccessful. After many years had passed, another King's son came by and heard the story of the sleeping Princess. He was not to be daunted by the failure of those who had gone before him.

It happened that one hundred years had very nearly passed since the great sleep had fallen on the castle. As this young Prince approached the thick, bramble hedge, the thorns turned into fine flowers and parted to let him through.

In the courtyard he saw the horses and dogs lying fast asleep. He stepped over the bodies of the courtiers in the Great Hall and saw the King and Queen asleep on their thrones.

The Prince looked in all the rooms in the castle, and at last he came to the tower and opened the door of the little chamber where the Princess slept. She looked so beautiful that the Prince

could not help but gaze upon her, and he bent down and kissed her. Just as he did so, she opened her eyes and smiled at him.

Then the King and Queen awoke, and the whole court, the servants, the horses, the dogs and the flies on the wall. The fire in the hearth began to burn brightly. The whole castle was once more alive with the sound of happy voices as if nothing had happened, for the hundred years sleep had made no difference to anyone.

Very soon, the wedding of The Prince and his Sleeping Beauty was celebrated with great splendour, and they lived together happy and contented to the end of their lives.

The Wolf & the Seven Little Goats

ILLUSTRATED BY KATE DAVIES

Once upon a time there lived a Nanny Goat who had seven young kids. She loved them as any mother loves her children. One day, she wanted to go into the forest, so she called the little goats together and said, "Dear children, I am going away into the wood; be on your guard against the wolf. If he comes here, he will eat you all up.

He may try to fool you into thinking he is someone else, but you will know him by his gruff voice and his black feet." "Don't worry, mother," the little goats replied, "we'll remember." So she went on her way, quite happily. Not long after the mother goat had gone, there was a knock at the door and a voice called out, "Open the door, children; your mother is here and has brought something for each of you."

But the little goats knew from the gruff voice that it was the wolf, so they said, "No, you cannot come in, you are not our mother. She has a kind and gentle voice, but yours is gruff; you are a wolf." So the wolf went home and found a piece of chalk, which he ate. This made his voice more gentle, so he returned to the goats' house, knocked at the door and called out, "Open, my dear children; your mother has come home and brought you each something." But the wolf had placed his paws on the window sill.

When the little goats saw them they said, "No, no, we will not open the door to you. Our mother has white paws, and yours are black. You are a wolf."

So the wolf went to a baker and said, "I have hurt my foot, put some dough on it." When the baker had done this, the wolf ran to the miller saying, "Put some white flour on my feet." But the miller, thinking the wolf was planning to fool someone, refused. But then the wolf said to him, "If you do not do what I ask, I will eat you." The miller was afraid, and powdered the wolf's feet with flour. Now, the wicked wolf went for a third time to the goats' house and knocked on the door. "Open up to me dear children; your mother is come, and I have brought you something nice from the forest."

He put his paws up on the window sill, and when the little goats saw that they were white, they thought it was safe, and they undid the door. Then who should come in but the wolf! They were so frightened, they ran and hid themselves. One ran under the table, the second crawled under the bed, the third hid in the cupboard, the fourth behind the kitchen door, the fifth in the oven, the sixth in the wash tub and the seventh in the big grandfather clock.

The wolf found them out, and quickly swallowed them up, one after the other; the only little goat he did not discover was in the grandfather clock.

The wolf could hardly move, but dragged himself into the forest, where he lay down to sleep. Soon the little goats' mother came home. What a terrible sight greeted her. The door was wide open; the table, stools and benches were overturned, the wash tub was broken in pieces, and the sheets were pulled off the bed. She

could not find her children anywhere.

She called them all by name, but they did not appear, until she came to the name of the youngest: "Here I am, mother, in the grandfather clock." When the little one came out, she told her mother what the wolf had done, and they hugged each

other and cried. They went out for a walk in the forest, and they came to a glade where they found the wolf sleeping. The mother goat walked right round the wolf as he lay there snoring, and she thought she saw something moving inside him.

"Oh my goodness!" she whispered to herself, "could it be that my poor children are still alive?"

They ran home to fetch a pair of scissors, needle and thread. Then the mother cut open the wicked wolf's hairy coat and out popped a little head. One little goat jumped out, followed by another, then another, until all six were set free. Not one of them was hurt, because the greedy monster had swallowed them all whole!

They danced and sang and hugged each other, and their mother said, "Quickly, go and fetch as many stones as you can find, so we can fill up the wolf's stomach before he wakes up." They gathered a pile of huge stones, and put them into his stomach. Their mother sewed up the slit with the needle and thread, and all the while, the greedy wolf did not stir.

When at last he woke up, he was very thirsty and went to a stream to have a drink. But as he rolled along from side to side, the stones tumbled about inside his body and he cried out:

"What rattles, what rattles

Against my poor bones?

Not little goats, I think,

But only big stones!"

When the wolf reached the edge of the stream he bent down to take a drink, and the heavy stones made him lose his balance, so that he fell, and sank beneath the water. All the while the little goats and their mother were watching from behind the trees. When they saw the big splash, they came running up, singing, "The wolf is dead! the wolf is dead!" and they danced for joy around their mother by the side of the stream.

Old Mother Frost

ILLUSTRATED BY STEPHEN ANGEL

There was once a widow who had two daughters. Her step-daughter was pretty and hard-working. The other was ugly and lazy.

The widow was kinder towards the ugly girl, because she was her own daughter, and she made the pretty girl do all the chores. The poor maiden was forced out every day to sit at the roadside by a well to spin.

She spun so much she made her fingers bleed. One day she bled so badly that the spindle became covered in blood, and she tried to wash it in the water in the well. As she leaned over, she accidentally let go and the spindle dropped into the water and sank to the bottom. The maiden ran crying to her stepmother who scolded her and said, "As you were the one to let the spindle fall into the well, you must go in after it and get it out again."

The poor girl went back to the well in despair and, not knowing what else she could do, jumped right into the well to get the spindle out. As she tumbled, she felt as though she had entered into a dream-like sleep and awoke to find herself in a beautiful meadow, where the sun was shining, birds were singing and thousands of flowers bloomed all around her.

Before her was a path and she followed it until she came to a baker's where the oven was full of bread. The loaves cried out to her, "Take me out, take me out, or I shall be burned, for I have been baked long enough."

So one by one, she took the loaves out of the oven. The maiden walked on further, until she came to an apple tree laden with ripe fruit which called out to her, "Shake us, shake us, for we are all ripe!" So she shook the tree until they had all fallen, and then she gathered them into a great heap and continued on her path.

At last she reached a cottage, and at the window she could see an old woman looking out at her. She had very large teeth, and the girl was frightened at the sight of her, and turned tail and ran. But the old woman called out to her, "Do not be afraid, child, but come and stay with me, and put my house in order.

All things will go well for you, as long as you make my bed properly, and shake it well so that all the feathers fly. Then it will snow upon the earth, for I am Old Mother Frost." The old woman had such a kind voice, that the maiden took courage, and agreed to stay with her and serve her. Every day she shook her bed so that the feathers blew down like flakes of snow, so the girl's life was happy, and the old woman saw to it that she was well fed and cared for.

The girl stayed with the old woman for a long time, but then she started to feel sad. At first she could not tell why she felt so sad, but after a while she knew that it was because she was homesick.

Even though her life here was so much better, she still longed to be back in her own home. "I would like to go home," she said to her mistress, "and if it does not go as well with me below as up here, then I will have to return."

"I could tell that you were homesick," said Old Mother Frost, "and as you have served me so well, when you decide you want to return, I shall bring you back here myself."

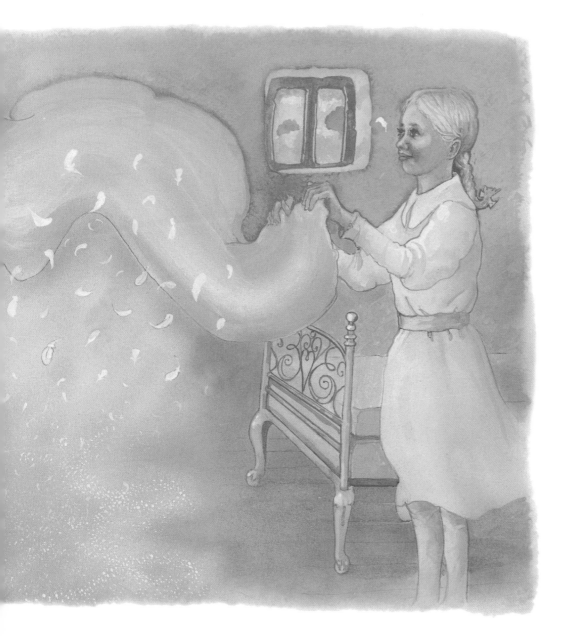

She led the maiden to a door in the loft which she unlatched, and when the girl was standing beneath it, a shower of gold fell down on her, and much of it stuck to her. "This is your reward for all your hard work," said the old woman, handing her the spindle which she had dropped into the well.

The door was closed, and immediately the maiden found herself standing outside her old home. She went in to her stepmother, and because she was covered in gold, she was not scolded for her long absence. The maiden told her story, and when the stepmother heard how she had come to possess all this gold, she decided to send her lazy, ugly daughter to try her luck. So she sent the girl to sit beside the well and spin. The lazy girl pricked her finger on a thorn to mark the spindle with her blood, dropped it into the well and dived in.

She found herself in the same beautiful meadow and followed the same path. When she came upon the baker's and heard the bread calling out, "Take me out, take me out, or I shall be burned, for I have been baked long enough," she replied, "I'm not going to dirty my hands to help you."

When she came to the apple tree laden with ripe fruit which called out to her, "Shake us, shake us, for we are all ripe!" she said, "Why don't you just fall and let me catch one of you?" She continued along the path until she came to Old Mother Frost's cottage.

194

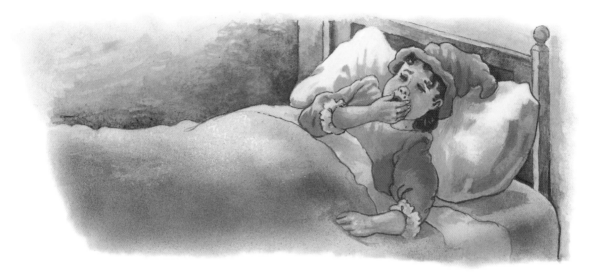

She was not afraid when she saw the teeth, as she had been warned, and she soon agreed to serve the old woman. Thinking of the gold that she would earn, the girl worked hard and well on the first day. But on the second she began to idle; on the third, even more so; until she would not get out of bed in the mornings. She did not make the beds as she should have, so the feathers did not fly. The old woman dismissed the lazy girl from her service, and as she led her to the door, the girl grew very excited, thinking, "Now the gold shower will come."

But when she stood under the door, instead of gold, there came upon her a shower of tar. "That is your reward for your service," said the old woman, and shut the door. The lazy girl came home to her mother's house, and she remained covered in tar for as long as she lived.

The Frog Prince

ILLUSTRATED BY IVANA SVABIC CANNON

Long ago there lived a king with several beautiful
daughters. But the youngest was so beautiful that even the
Sun himself was enchanted when she came out to play in
the sunshine. She would often go out into the garden by herself,
and one afternoon she was dancing around on the grass, throwing
a golden ball up into the air and catching it again.

The ball glinted in the sunshine and the Princess missed catching it when for a moment the bright light blinded her eyes.

She laughed as she ran down the slope chasing after it. Then she threw the golden ball high into the air and watched in horror as it fell into a well so deep that it seemed to take forever before she heard a feint plop as it hit the water at the bottom.

The Princess sat down beside the well and wept. She cried louder and louder until she heard a voice call out, "Why are you crying O King's daughter? Your tears would melt even a stone to pity." She looked around to the spot where the voice was coming from and saw a Frog's ugly face staring at her.

"Was it you that spoke? I am weeping for my golden ball which has fallen into this well and I don't know how I will ever get it back." "Never mind," said the Frog, "I can get it back for you. But what will you give me if I do?" "What would you like, dear Frog? You can have my jewels, my pearls or my golden crown." "I have no use for these things," replied the Frog, "but if you will love me, and let me play with you, sit at your table, eat from your plate, drink from your cup, and sleep in your bed, then I will climb into the well and retrieve your golden ball."

"Oh, I will promise you all these things, if only I can have my ball," she cried, thinking that she would never have to keep a promise she made to a Frog. But the Frog dropped into the well, picked up the golden ball in his mouth and climbed all the way out. The Princess thanked him, took the ball and ran off, as fast as she could, back to the palace. "Stop! Stop! Wait for me! I cannot keep up with you," croaked the Frog in his loudest voice, but she did not even hear him.

The Princess soon forgot the Frog and the promise she had made, and the frog hopped back into the lake near the well. One day, the King's daughter was sitting at table with her father and his courtiers when she heard a knock at the door. She went to open it and there before her stood the Frog. The Princess turned very pale and quickly shut the door. As she sat down to eat again her father asked her if there was a giant at the door to frighten

her so. "No father, it is not a giant, but an ugly Frog." "And what does the Frog want?" said the King. The Princess told her father the story of how she lost her golden ball in the well and the promise she made to the Frog. Then the King said, "A promise made must be kept.

Go and let him in." So reluctantly she went and opened the door and the Frog followed her back to her place. "Pick me up," he said, and the King ordered her to obey. She placed the Frog on her chair, and immediately he sprang up onto the table and demanded, "Move your plate close to me and we will eat together."

Everyone at the table could see she was very unwilling, but she did what she had promised. The Frog relished every mouthful but the King's daughter felt sick and could not eat any more of her food. When she got down from the table she lifted the Frog

onto the floor and he followed her
out into the garden to play. The
little Frog went everywhere with
her and when she thought she could
escape from him, she ran as fast as
she could back to the palace.
Remembering her promise that
she would let the Frog sleep in
her bed, she ran straight upstairs
to her bedroom and
bolted the door. Just as
the Princess got into
bed, she heard a feint
knocking sound.

"Who's there?" she called, her voice trembling. "Please let me in; you promised I could sleep in your bed, and your father said a promise made must be kept." The Princess opened the door and the Frog hopped across the room and clambered up onto the bed. The frightened girl curled up as far away from the Frog as she could, but was unable to sleep all night.

The next day, the little Frog refused to leave the Princess's side. He played with her, sat on her lap when she rode with her father in his carriage and ate from her plate at meal times. The poor girl was growing tired of this ugly little creature and feared she might never be rid of him. "Will you never go away and leave me alone, you ugly little Frog?" she asked him tearfully. "First, you must kiss me, and then if you really want me to leave you sweet Princess, I will go." Kiss a Frog? The poor girl thought she would rather die. But so desperate was she to be free of him that she took a deep breath, closed her eyes, and offered him   her lips to kiss.

When she opened her eyes she found that the Frog had indeed disappeared, and in his place stood a tall, handsome young Prince.

He told her how a wicked witch had transformed him and that only she could set him free from the spell. She fell in love with him instantly and they ran back to the palace to find her father. He gave his consent to their marriage and the Prince and Princess lived very happily in his kingdom for many years.

The Fisherman and his Wife

ILLUSTRATED BY KEN OLIVER

Once upon a time there was a fisherman and his wife who live in a little hut by the sea. Every day he took his rod to the pier and waited to see what he caught on the end of the line. One morning he felt a tug on the line and and when he drew it up a huge Flounder was hooked on it.

The Flounder said, "Please let me go, fisherman, for I am not a real fish, but an enchanted Prince. I will not be good to eat." So the fisherman let the flounder go. Then he got up, and went home to his wife. "Have you caught nothing today, husband," she said. "Oh," he replied, "I caught a Flounder, but he said he was an enchanted Prince, and I let him go."

"What? Did you not first make a wish?" she asked. "No," said he. "And why not? Do you wish to remain in this hovel for ever? Go back and catch him again so you can make a wish. Tell him that I would like a cottage with a little garden."

The fisherman was not very pleased with his wife for asking him to do this, but he went back to the place where he had caught the Flounder. The water looked green and yellow, and as he gazed into it the Flounder poked his head out.

"What do you want with me?" asked the Fish. "Oh," said the man, I was to catch you again, for my wife says that I should have wished before. She will not live any longer in our hovel and desires a cottage.""Return to her and you will find that she has her wish," said the Flounder, and he swam off.

When the fisherman got home he found in place of his hut a pretty cottage with a garden. His wife led him inside and showed him the pretty furnishings, the stone sink, the stove and bright, shiny copper pans. She took him outside to show him the garden full of vegetables and fruit trees. "Yes," said her husband, "if it continues to bloom, you will be very happy.""We will think about that," she replied, and they went to bed.

A week or two passed by and the woman said to her husband, "This cottage is not big enough for me. The Flounder might give us a bigger house. I wish to live in a stone palace. Go and tell him to give us a castle." "Ah, wife," said he, "surely a cottage is enough for us. Why do you want to live in a castle?"

"Off you go, now," she said, "the Flounder can easily give you that." "But he might be angry with me if I ask him for anything else," pleaded the fisherman. "Don't worry," said she, "it will be easy for him to give it." So the fisherman set off again and came to the place where he had seen the Flounder. The water looked clouded and a deep shade of blue, and as the fisherman gazed into it, the Flounder's head popped out of it. "Now then, what do you want?" he asked.

"Oh, my wife wants to live in a stone castle," said the man, his voice trembling with fear.

"Go home and you will find her in it," said the Flounder. The fisherman went back to the place by the sea where the cottage had stood, but found instead a great stone castle. His wife was waiting on the steps, ready to meet him and show him round their new home.

There was a great hall with long tables and many servants ready to cook, serve, clean and garden for them. There were rooms hung with tapestries and filled with fine golden chairs and crystal mirrors on the walls. Outside were large courtyards and stables with horses and the finest carriages. The gardens were filled with flowers and fruit trees, and in the meadows all around they could see cattle, sheep and deer, as many as anyone could wish for.

"Isn't this so pretty?" said the wife. "Ah, you will be content with this for a while, and then you will want something else," said the fisherman. "We will think about that," she replied, and they went to bed.

The very next day the wife was looking out of her window while her husband was still asleep. She woke him and said, "Look out of this window and think, shall I not be Queen over all the land?

Go to the Flounder and tell him that we want to be King and Queen." "Ah, wife," said he, "Why should I wish to be King." "No," she replied, "you do not wish, so I will be Queen. Go and tell the Flounder."

So the fisherman went back to the pier and gazed into the water. This time it looked quite black and smelled bad. Then the Flounder's head popped out of the water and he said, "What does she want now?" "Ah!" said he, "she wants to be Queen." "Return to her now, for she already is," said the Fish. When the man reached the castle, he found it much larger, with a herald standing before a gateway, and many soldiers. Inside everything was made of gold and marble.

Beyond the great hall sat his wife on a gold and diamond throne with a jewelled crown on her head. Six page boys stood on her left, and six on her right.

Then he went up to her and said, "Ah, wife, are you Queen now?" "Yes," said she, "I am Queen!" He looked at her for a long time and said, "So now you will be content?" "No, no," she replied, "I am not at all satisfied with being Queen. I want to be Pope. Go and tell the Flounder that I want to be Pope."

"Oh, wife, how can you even think of being Pope? He is the head of Christendom." "I will be Pope, I will" replied the wife, stamping her feet and shaking her fist.

The poor fisherman had no choice; he had to go back to the Flounder. When he came to the shore, the waves were high and the sky was black. Terrified, he called out to the Flounder.

"What is it now?" asked the Flounder. "She wants to be Pope." "Go home and you will find her so," So he went back and found her in a great church, sitting on a much higher throne with Kings and Queens bowing before her.

"Now you must be content," said he, "as you are Pope, and there is nothing else you can be." "We will think about that," said she, and they went to bed. She awoke early the next morning and watched the sun rising. She thought to herself, "Why should I not do that?"

So she woke her husband and told him, "Go to the Flounder and tell him I want to make the sun rise." The poor man was too frightened to argue with her, and still in his nightshirt, went down to the sea.

A fierce storm was raging and he could not hear himself shouting out to the Flounder. "What does she want now?" asked the fish. "She wants to be Ruler of the Universe." "Go and find her back in her hovel," replied the Flounder. And there the fisherman and his wife lived for the rest of their days.

Snow White & the Seven Dwarfs

ILLUSTRATED BY DAVID LONG

It was the middle of winter. A Queen sat by a window made of the finest black ebony. As she looked out at the snow, she pricked her finger and three drops of blood fell onto it.

She gazed at the red drops in the white snow and said, "I wish my little daughter to be as white as the snow, as red as blood and as black as ebony ."

And her daughter was beautiful, with skin as white as snow, cheeks as rosy as the blood, and hair as black as ebony. Her name was Snow White.

Sadly the Queen died, and Snow White's father married another wife. This Queen had a magic mirror. She would gaze at herself and say,

"Mirror, mirror, on the wall,
   Who is the fairest of them all?"
And the mirror would reply,
   "You, O Queen, are the fairest in
      the land."

But one day, when she looked into the mirror, it answered her,

"You my Queen, may lovely be
But Snow White is by far the most beautiful in the land."

The Queen called one of her servants and ordered him to take Snow White out into the woods. "I never want to see her again", she screeched! The servant was very unhappy and did not want to hurt Snow White. So he left her in the wood, and returned to the Queen to tell her that Snow White was dead.

Poor Snow White was alone and afraid as she wandered in the wood. As night fell, she reached a cottage.

It was the home of seven dwarfs. Inside, she found a table neatly laid with seven small loaves of bread and seven little glasses of wine. Against the wall were seven small beds.

Snow White was very hungry, so she helped herself to a little bread from each loaf, and a sip of wine from each glass. Then she lay down and fell asleep.

When they returned from their day's work, the seven dwarfs were not at all pleased with the mess that they saw on the table.

They turned around and found Snow White sleeping soundly.

At first they grumbled and complained to one another, but then, they all gazed in amazement at her beauty, and agreed to let her sleep until morning.

Snow White stayed with the dwarfs. While they were hard at work in the Diamond Mine, she looked after their cottage and prepared the meals every day. One day, the Queen looked into her mirror and asked her usual question.

The mirror replied;
   "You are the fairest in this place.
   But by far the most beautiful face
   Belongs to Snow White."
         The Queen was furious. "I thought she was
      dead!" she cried. She disguised herself
         as an old gypsy woman and went
            off into the woods in search of
            Snow White. She carried
            with her a basket of
            apples. One of the
            apples was poisoned
            on one side. When
            she came upon the
            cottage, she knocked
            on the door.
               Snow White
            opened the window,
            looked out and said,
         "I dare not let anyone in."

"Never mind dear. Just let me give you one of my beautiful apples." Snow White did not want to take it, but the Queen said, "Look, I will take a bite and you will see that it is safe."

Snow White then took a bite of the apple and fell down dead. When the dwarfs returned from work that day they were very unhappy to find Snow White lying lifeless on the ground. She was so beautiful and they wanted to look at her forever, so they laid her in a glass coffin.

Snow White looked as if she were only sleeping. One day a prince rode by and begged the dwarfs to let him take Snow White away with him. They refused at first, but then they took pity on him, and granted his wish. As soon as he lifted the coffin, a piece of apple fell from Snow White's lips, and she awoke.

The Prince asked Snow White to go with him to his father's palace and marry him.

The wicked Queen was invited to the marriage feast, and when she arrived and saw that Snow White was the bride, she choked with rage, fell ill and died. But Snow White and the Prince reigned happily over that land for many, many years.

The King's New Clothes

ILLUSTRATED BY JAN NESBITT

235

Many years ago there lived a King who was very rich and liked nothing more than buying new clothes. He did not enjoy hunting, or going to the theatre, except that these occasions gave him the chance to show off his latest outfits. Time passed away merrily in the town where the King had his castle home, and every day people visited his court. One day two men, calling themselves weavers, asked to see the King.

They told him how they knew how to weave materials of the most beautiful colours and patterns, and how the clothes made from these materials were invisible to all who were unfit for the office they held, as well as to those who were exceptionally stupid.

"These must be splendid clothes," thought the King to himself, "and it will be useful to know who in my kingdom is wise, and who is stupid, and who is unfit for the office they hold." "Yes, make me a fine suit of clothes from this fabric," said the King, and he ordered a large sum of money to be given to the two men, so that they might start work at once.

The rogues asked to be supplied with vast quantities of the finest silk and gold thread, which they hid in the cellars of their houses. Then they set up a workshop with two looms, and pretended to work at weaving the amazing cloth.

Everyone in the city heard about the suit of clothes that was being made for the King, and they were all anxious to learn how wise, or indeed how foolish, their neighbours would turn out to be. Not to mention who would be found to be unfit for the office they held.

"I should like to know how the weavers are getting on with my cloth," thought the King one day. But he was a little nervous about going to have a look himself, for he thought it possible that he might be found to be stupid, or unfit to be King.

So he decided to send his faithful old minister, "for he is a man of good sense, and if anyone is fit for his office, it is he," said the King. So the faithful old minister went to see the weavers, and found them working away at the empty looms. "What does this mean?" he said to himself, for he could see no fabric.

"Could it be that I am stupid, or even not fit for my office? I must pretend that I can see it." "Come closer," said one of the knaves, and look at the pattern. Is it not beautiful?" "Yes," replied the old minister, "it is excellent. I will tell his Majesty today just how beautiful it is."

They talked at length about the pattern and the colours, and the minister listened carefully to every word so he could tell the King exactly what it looked like. Then the two men asked for more silk and gold thread to be brought to them, so they could finish making the fabric. They hid these in the cellars of their houses, and continued to pretend to work at the empty looms.

A few days later, the King sent another of his officers to see when the cloth would be ready. When he saw the empty looms he also decided to pretend that he could see the cloth, not wanting anyone to know that he was either stupid, or not fit to hold his profitable office.

So when the two men asked him, "Are you not delighted with the colours and the pattern?" he replied,"Yes, it is very beautiful," and he too listened carefully to their descriptions. He returned to the King with a detailed account of the fabric.

Soon the whole city was talking about the remarkable cloth that was being woven especially for the King. And now the King himself decided to go and examine it.

He selected a number of courtiers to accompany him, including the two who had already admired the cloth.

The men appeared to be working hard at the empty looms as the royal party entered the room. The two officers, imagining everyone else could see the fabric on the loom, declared, "Look at these patterns, look at these colours; is it not magnificent?"

"Oh dear," thought the King, "how can this be? I can see nothing. I cannot let anyone think that I am a fool, or that I am unfit to be King." So he said, "It is amazing! I must have a suit of clothes made from this fabric to wear for the procession."

And all his courtiers applauded this decision, even though not one of them could see anything at all.

It was not many days before the grand royal procession was due to take place in the city, and the tricksters sat up late every night, pretending to cut and pin and sew. "Look!" they cried at last, "the King's new clothes are ready."

The courtiers gathered to escort the King to the chamber where the rogues were waiting to dress him in his new suit. As he entered, they raised their arms as if they were holding something up, saying, "Here is your coat, your Majesty," and "Here are your trousers. This is the shirt, and these are the fine undergarments you will need to put on. The whole suit is so light that when you wear it you will feel as though you are wearing nothing at all!"

Not one of the courtiers could see a thing, yet they all declared how exquisite the garments appeared.

"If your Majesty will be pleased to take off your clothes, we will fit your new suit."

The King was undressed by his personal servants and stood in front of a mirror while the two rogues pretended to put on the new suit.

"How splendid his Majesty looks," cried out the courtiers, "and how well the clothes fit,"

"The colours are beautiful," said one, "the design is magnificent,"said another, as the King turned from side to side, admiring himself in the mirror. Out in the streets all the people were talking about the King's amazing new suit. There was great excitement as they took their places, wondering who would be found to be wise and who among them were fools.

Meanwhile, at the palace, the King smoothed down his imaginary coat and his courtiers busied themselves arranging the train on the floor behind him. Then six of them pretended to pick it up and walked proudly behind the King. A crown was placed on his head, and he set off on his grand procession through the streets.

The people gasped as they saw him approach, and cried out, "Your clothes are beautiful!" Not one of them could see a stitch on the King, but they did not want to appear foolish in front of the King or their fellow citizens.

Those who held office, high and low, were mindful of losing their positions in life, so they were not willing to confess to what they really saw.

But there was a little boy in the crowd who had not heard the story about the King's magic suit of clothes, and as the grand procession came into view, the child let out a piercing shriek and cried, "Look at the King! Look at the King! The King has got no clothes on!"

Another voice was heard to say, "The King has got no clothes on!" And then another, and another until the whole town was filled with laughter as they all realised that they had been tricked.

Everyone except the King and his officers was laughing. The poor man walked on in a most dignified manner, with those following holding up the imaginary train until they reached the safety of the palace.

What became of the two tricksters? Well, the instant that the King and his party had left the palace, they raced home, emptied the cellar of their treasure and loaded it onto a cart. By the time the grand procession was over they had escaped into another kingdom, and they lived there in the lap of luxury for the rest of their days.

The Little Match Girl

ILLUSTRATED BY STEPHEN ANGEL

It was New Year's Eve. A poor little girl, barefoot, hungry and cold, was wandering the dark streets. She carried a bundle of matches, but no one had bought any from her that day. No one had even tossed her a coin.

The snowflakes settled on her long, fair curly hair. Lights were shining from every window in the town, and the smell of roast goose wafted into the freezing night air. She sat down in a sheltered corner between two houses, hugging her knees to her chest, but she could not get herself warm.

The little match girl did not dare to go home. She knew her father would surely beat her, as she had not earned a penny. Besides, her home was nearly as cold as it was on the street. Her hands were very nearly frozen. If she could light a match, maybe she could warm them. She pulled one out, and struck it against the wall beside her. It gave a bright, warm light, like a little candle, and she held her hands over it. It was a wonderful light.

The poor little girl felt as though she were sitting in front of a large iron stove. So beautifully did the fire burn, that she stretched out her feet to warm them also.

Sadly, in an instant, the flame died away, leaving her cold and comfortless. She struck another match, and wherever the light from this one fell, the wall of the house became transparent, and the little girl could see right into the room.

She saw the table spread with a snowy-white cloth and laid with the finest china.

At one end of the table, smoking hot, was a roast goose, stuffed with apples and prunes. The little girl saw the goose jump down from the table, and waddle along the floor until it stood in front of her. Then, the match burned out, and she only saw the thick, hard wall beside her.

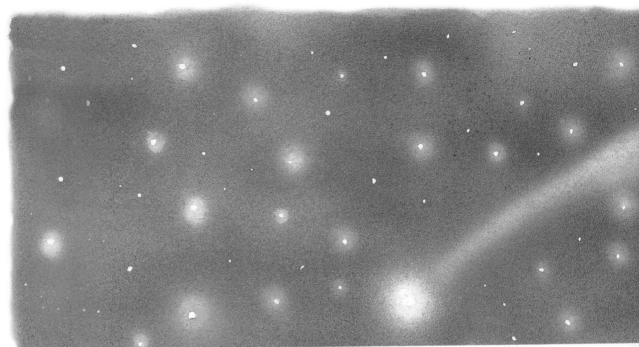

So she lit a third match. Again the flame shot up, and now she was sitting under a beautiful Christmas tree. Thousands of little candles glowed in the branches, and tiny painted figures looked down on her.

As the little girl reached out towards the figures, the match went out. But still, the Christmas candles burned higher and higher, until they looked like stars in the sky. One of the stars fell, the light streaming behind it like a fiery tail.

"Now someone is dying," said the little girl softly, for she had been told by her old grandmother, the only person who had ever been kind to her, but was now dead, that when a star falls from the sky, a soul flies up to God.

The little girl struck another match against the wall, and in the brightness of the light shining around her, she saw her grandmother, gentle and loving as always, but bright and happy as she had never looked during her lifetime.

"Oh Grandmother!" cried the little girl, "take me with you! I know you will leave me as soon as the match goes out.

You will vanish like the warm stove, like the New Year's feast, and like the beautiful Christmas tree." And she quickly lit all the matches in the bundle. They burned brighter than the noonday sun. The good old grandmother took the little girl in her arms, and they both flew away together radiant with happiness.

They flew higher and higher, far above the earth, till they reached that place where neither cold, nor hunger, nor pain is ever known - in the presence of God. But in the cold light of dawn, curled up beside the wall, the poor little match girl was found, frozen to death.

The burned out matches lay in her lap. "She has been
trying to warm herself, poor thing," someone said. But no one
knew of the beautiful visions she had seen, or how gloriously she
and her grandmother were celebrating the New Year in heaven!

The Golden Goose

ILLUSTRATED BY BRIAN ROBERTSON

There was once a man who had three sons, the youngest of whom was named Dummling. People made fun of Dummling because of his name, and thought him stupid. One day his eldest brother wanted to go into the forest to cut wood, and his mother gave him a large pancake and a bottle of wine to take with him.

On his journey he met an old man who wished him good-day

and said, "Give me a piece of your pancake and a sip of your wine for I am hungry and thirsty." "If I give you my cake and wine, there will not be enough for me," said the eldest son, and went on his way. He began to cut down a tree, but after a few strokes, he missed his aim, and hurt his arm. So he had to go home.

Afterwards the second son went off into the forest. His mother gave him a pancake and a bottle of wine, just like his brother. He met the same old man, who asked him politely for a little piece of cake and a sip of wine. "If I give you my cake and wine, there will not be enough for me," said the second son, and went on his way. He began to cut down a tree, but after a few strokes, he missed his aim, and hurt his leg. So he had to go home.

Then Dummling asked his father if he could go into the forest to cut wood, but his father said:

"No, you don't know how to do it properly. Look what happened to your brothers. You will surely hurt yourself." But Dummling begged for so long to be allowed to go, that his father finally agreed. His mother sent him away with a small cake that had been baked in

the ashes, and a bottle of sour beer. Dummling was met by the same old man who greeted him and said, "Give me a piece of cake and a sip of your drink, for I am hungry and thirsty."

Dummling replied, "I have only a cake baked in ashes and a bottle of sour beer, but you are most welcome to share it with me." And as Dummling took out his cake, he found in his hand the most delicious pancake to share with the old man, and the sour beer had become wine. The old man said to him, "As you are so generous, I will make you lucky. Cut down that tree over there."

So Dummling did as the old man had told him, and when the tree fell, he saw at its roots a goose which had feathers of pure gold. He picked up the Golden Goose and set off for home.

On the way he stopped at an inn. The innkeeper had three daughters who stared longingly at Dummling's goose, and each girl waited for an opportunity to steal just one of its feathers.

At last, the eldest girl saw her chance, but as she touched the goose, she found herself stuck fast to its wing, and she could not break free. The second girl thought she could pluck a feather, but as she touched her sister's arm, she could not pull her hand away. They cried out to the youngest sister, "Keep away! Keep away!" But greed got the better of her and as she tried to grasp a feather she stuck fast to her sisters. Dummling continued his journey with the goose under his arm and the three girls still hanging on.

They were met by a parson who scolded the girls, saying, "Why are you running after that young man across the fields?" And as he reached out to grab the hand of the youngest to pull her away, he stuck to her and had to follow in the procession.

The parson's clerk saw his master in difficulty and took hold of his gown, and now there were five following behind Dummling and the Golden Goose. The parson and the clerk

called out for help, and when two woodcutters came to their aid, they too were stuck fast, and so there were seven following behind Dummling and the Golden Goose.

It happened that at that time, the King in this country had a daughter, his only child, who never smiled or laughed.

The King decreed that any man who could make her laugh would marry her.

Princes came with their jesters from far and wide, but none of them could extract a smile from her lips.

But when Dummling, with his Golden Goose under his arm, and the seven poor creatures trotting along one behind the other passed by her window, the princess just laughed and laughed. Dummling went to the King and demanded his bride, but the King thought him too simple a man to be his son-in-law, and made excuses.

Eventually, the King sent Dummling away with another task. "If you can bring me a ship which will travel on land and water, then you shall have my daughter for your bride."

Dummling went into the forest and found the old man who had shared his food and drink.

He told his story, and the old man, remembering his promise to make him lucky, gave Dummling a vessel which could travel on both land and water, with these words: "Since I have eaten and drunk with you, I give you the ship. And all this I do because you are so good natured."

As soon as the King saw the ship, he could no longer hold back his daughter from Dummling and the wedding was celebrated. When the King died, Dummling inherited the kingdom, and lived happily with his bride for many years.